RJ'S CREEPY TALES

CAMP TOXIC

"You won't be glowing home!"

Shawn Rumley, Jasin Harms, and Joe Rumley

PAGE PUBLISHING, INC.
Conneaut Lake, PA

First originally published by Page Publishing 2020

ISBN 978-1-64628-986-8 (pbk)
ISBN 978-1-64544-231-8 (hc)
ISBN 978-1-64544-228-8 (digital)

Printed in the United States of America

I am writing a dedication page to; Jim and Cheryl Rumley, my mom and dad, and Ruth Rumley, my Grandma.

Thanks to those that helped including Samuel Hans, Josh Fiorini, Ginny Whitebread, Ashley Nicole, Andrea Blair, Emma Rumley, Ava Rumley, Joell Olalde Springman, and Robert Fielding.

Computer camp, where you stay up late playing video games, sleep till noon, and prank other kids, a place where there are no bullies. That was supposed to be my summer camp.

But did I get to go there? No! My parents sent me to Camp Toxic, a camp for bad kids, a camp full of bullies!

My name is Larry, and I'm here for hacking the school's computer and changing my grade in gym class from a D to an A. That guy is Butch. He's here for poisoning his whole town. Well…I think that's why he's here.

They call that man Sarge. He's the head man in charge here. He's the biggest bully of all.

The kids here are so bad they are already talking about sneaking out.

11

That's Jett, the camp prankster. He's known for all the big pranks done at this camp.

Someone had put a ton of Jell-O packages in to the water, turning Sarge's fishing hole into a Jell-O lake. Wade, the other camp counselor, tried to calm Sarge down.

Sarge was so upset someone ruined his fishing lake, he sent everyone to their cabins while he tried to fish in the Jell-O.

15

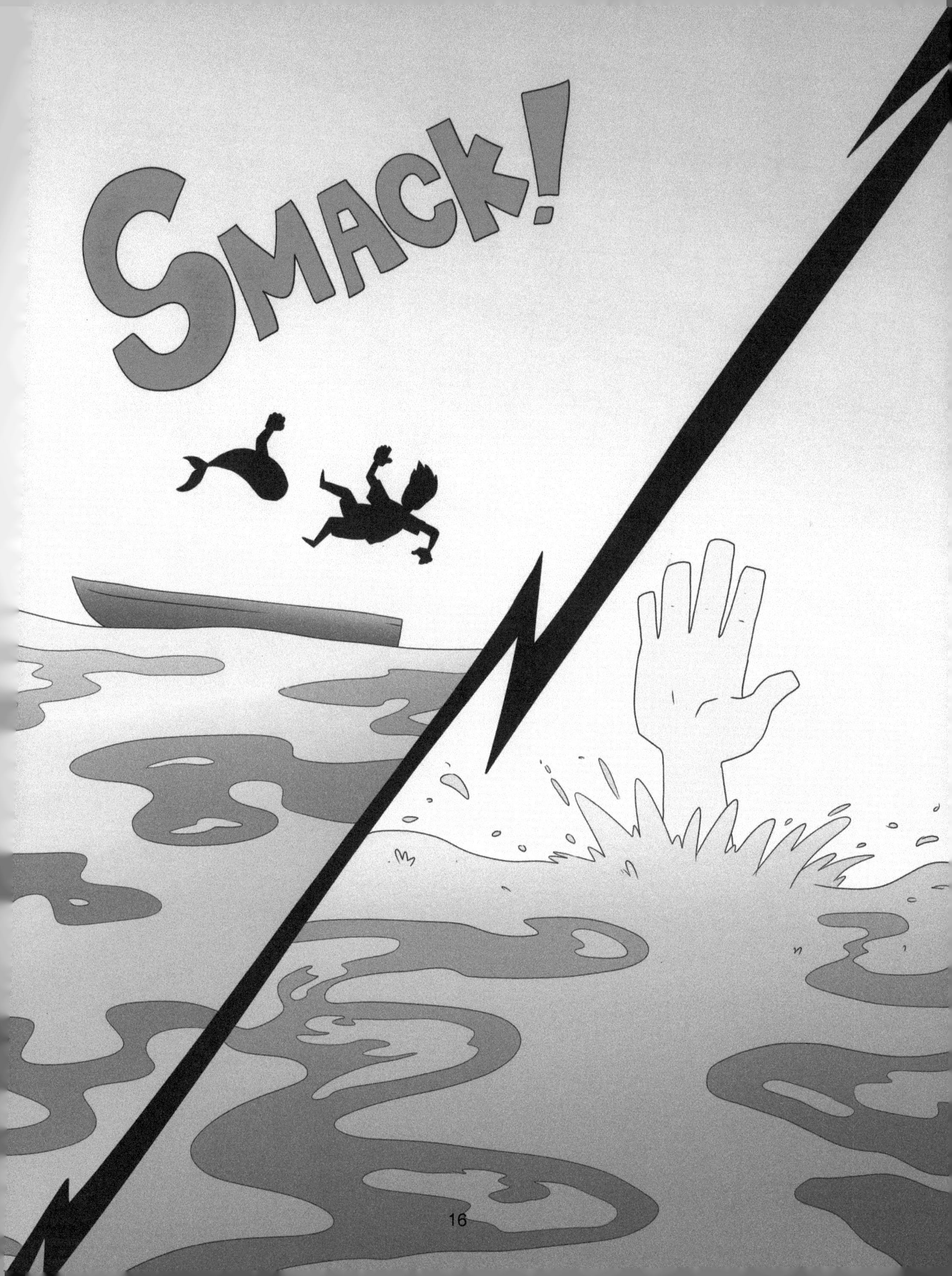
SMACK!

We haven't seen Sarge for a while, so we thought it was a good time to sneak out.

HELLO BOYS!
WHAT HAPPENED TO SARGE?
CAMP TOXIC
HE GOT MUTATED BY THE LAKE!

A glow-in-the-dark Sarge showed up as we were looking at the lake.

I think I ran faster than I ever did. When we got back to the cabin, we pushed the bunk beds against the door.

The next day, I woke up to a horrible smell—it was Butch's nasty foot in my face!

When we went to eat breakfast, Sarge was there. He was trying to make us eat this green glowing Jell-O that looked like it came straight from the lake. We could see worms in it!

Sarge went off the deep end. He smashed Butch's face in the Jell-O.

As Wade yelled at him, we ran to the cabin. Sarge was clearly not right. We had to get out of Camp Toxic before we became green freaks too.

We had a plan. We were going to get a good night's sleep and walk back to town the next day. Well…we had that plan until Sarge yanked us out of our beds in the middle of the night.

Just when we thought all was lost, Wade pulled up with the bus. Butch quickly shoved Sarge down, giving us time to get away.

When I got home, I was still mad my dad didn't get me home sooner.

Camp Toxic Sign-Up Sheet

Does your child act out? Is he or she mouthy? Do they not take out the trash when told, or do you just want a summer away from your brat? For any reason, you can sign your child up for Camp Toxic, they will come back changed or your money back guarantee. Sign your child up now, and get rid of that toxic behavior!

Name ....

Name ....

Name ....

Name ....

Permission Slip

TOXIC JELL-O RECIPE

Step 1: Purchase green Jell-O.

Step 2: Mix according to back of package.

Step 3: Put gummy worms or gummy fish in liquid Jell-O.

Step 4: Place Jell-O in fridge for the appropriate time.

Step 5: Enjoy.

Side effects include massive amounts of strength, pigment of skin turning green, possible glowing in the dark, teeth rotting, worms coming out of ears, and lots of energy. Now don't wait, hurry up and make your Toxic Jell-O with your parents today!

Coming soon:
Emma's Twisted Tales
Zombie Tablet
Welcome to Clown Town
Return to Camp Toxic
Summer School Nightmare
Day of the Cotton Candy Monster
My Pet Zombie
My Bus Driver Is an Alien
Night of the Hog Monster
The Toilet Monster
How Fast Can a Ghost Run
I Think My Dentist Is a Vampire
Christmas Troll

CPSIA information can be obtained
at www.ICGtesting.com
Printed in the USA
LVHW052230310720
662086LV00006B/74